CUTTING-EDGE TECHNO

ROBOTICS

Louise and Richard Spilsbury

Gareth Stevens
PUBLISHING

Please visit our website, **www.garethstevens.com**.
For a free color catalog of all our high-quality books,
call toll free 1-800-542-2595 or fax 1-877-542-2596.

Cataloging-in-Publication Data

Names: Spilsbury, Louise.
Title: Robotics / Louise and Richard Spilsbury.
Description: New York: Gareth Stevens Publishing, 2017. | Series: Cutting-edge technology | Includes index.
Identifiers: ISBN 9781482451665 (pbk.) | ISBN 9781482451603 (library bound) | ISBN 9781482451481 (6 pack)
Subjects: LCSH: Robotics–Juvenile literature.
Classification: LCC TJ211.2 S65 2017 | DDC 629.8'92–dc23

First Edition

Published in 2017 by
Gareth Stevens Publishing
111 East 14th Street, Suite 349
New York, NY 10003

© 2017 Gareth Stevens Publishing

Produced for Gareth Stevens by Calcium
Editors: Sarah Eason and Harriet McGregor
Designer: Jessica Moon
Picture researcher: Rachel Blount

Picture credits: Cover: Getty Images: ChinaFotoPress (photo), Shutterstock: Eky Studio (banner), Shutterstock: R-studio (back cover bkgrd); Inside: ARxIUM: 28; EKSO Bionics: 31; ESA: AOES 19; Fullwood Ltd.: Fullwood M²erlin 14; Intuitive Surgical: ©2009 Intuitive Surgical, Inc. 27; NASA: JPL-Caltech 21; NOAA: Flower Garden Banks National Marine Sanctuary/G.P. Schmahl 33; Shutterstock: Beerkoff 25, Chesky 43, Lonny Garris 9, Nataliya Hora 13, Kajornyot 35, Magicinfoto 45, MilanTomazin 41, Wellphoto 1, 11; Wikimedia Commons: DARPA 7, Sergei Kazantsev (CC-BY-SA-4.0) 5, NASA Ames Research Center 17, NASA/Expedition 39 23, OAR/National Undersea Research Program (NURP); Mass. Institute of Technology 37, Sgt. Sarah Dietz, U.S. Marine Corps 39.

Printed in the United States of America
CPSIA compliance information: Batch #CS16GS: For further information contact Gareth Stevens, New York, New York at 1-800-542-2595.

CONTENTS

CHAPTER 1

THE RISE OF ROBOTS

Robotics is all about designing, building, and operating robots. It involves the work of specialist engineers who find mechanical, electrical, and electronic solutions to problems in order to make robots for different purposes. Many people think of a robot as a mechanical being that looks a little like a human. However, robots have different shapes and sizes because they are created to do certain jobs.

ROBOTS IN REAL LIFE

Robots are far more than just machines like vacuum cleaners and lawn mowers. Some robots are critical lifesavers. They might be used to carry out surgery in hospitals or to accurately mix up drugs to make medicines. Other robots safely explode hidden bombs or transport dangerous materials. Others are used just for fun!

Industries use robots because they have advantages over human workers. A robot can be programmed to do a routine task over and over without stopping, in exactly the same way and in exactly the same period of time. People become tired or bored doing the same task repeatedly and for long periods. They may make mistakes or risk being injured at work. Robots can also be made from materials that do not get damaged by heat, **pressure**, chemicals, or sharp or explosive substances.

If they are programmed well, robotic devices can do tasks that usually require human thought. Here, a chess robot takes on several human players at once in Russia!

FIRST ROBOTS

In 1921, a new play opened in Prague, Czechoslovakia, and introduced the word "robot" to the world. In *Rossum's Universal Robots* by Karel Capek, the robots were mass-produced workers with no feelings. They did the jobs that people did not like to do. In the play, the robots take over the army, do all the jobs, and eventually rule the world!

Since the time of the ancient Greeks, people have dreamed of tools that carry out tasks without the need for operators. By the fifteenth century, Leonardo da Vinci (1452–1519) had made sketches of mechanical humans, but it was not until a few centuries later that working automatic machines were first developed.

AUTOMATIC MACHINES

One of the most famous early robot inventors was Jacques de Vaucanson (1709–1782). He built realistic, life-size models of people that could do things automatically, such as play the flute. His best-known automaton was the digesting duck, which could not only flap its wings, but also eat grain and digest it! Jacques later made machines to automatically weave silk fabric using information stored as patterns of holes on paper rolls.

ROBOTS ARRIVE

In the early 1960s, the first commercial robot started work in factories. Unimate was a robotic arm designed to remove and stack very hot disks of metal used to make cars. The arm was positioned in one place to carry out this one task. People controlled the robot by inputting **data** into a computer, which sent information to move its parts. Gradually, many types of arms took on more roles in factories. In the 1980s, Honda began to develop robots that looked and moved like humans. ASIMO is its most famous humanoid, or humanlike, robot. It resembles an astronaut 3 feet (1 m) high. This robot can run, walk up and down stairs, pick up and use objects, and respond to voice commands.

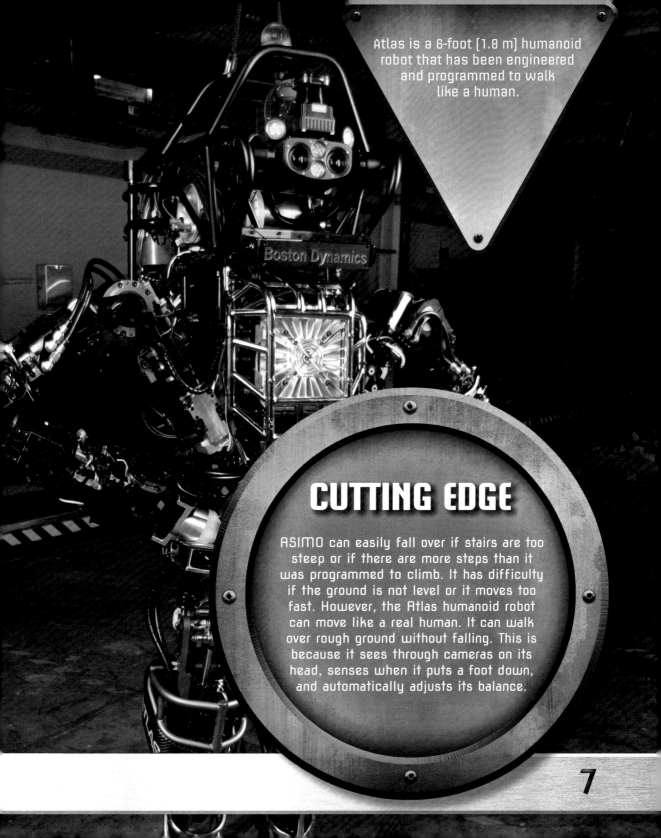

Atlas is a 6-foot (1.8 m) humanoid robot that has been engineered and programmed to walk like a human.

Boston Dynamics

CUTTING EDGE

ASIMO can easily fall over if stairs are too steep or if there are more steps than it was programmed to climb. It has difficulty if the ground is not level or it moves too fast. However, the Atlas humanoid robot can move like a real human. It can walk over rough ground without falling. This is because it sees through cameras on its head, senses when it puts a foot down, and automatically adjusts its balance.

ROBOTIC PARTS

Robotic devices can be tiny, such as an insect-sized flying **drone**, or huge like a giant industrial robotic arm or even a coal-mining machine. However, they share several basic parts that together allow them to function. The simplest way to understand the parts is to think of them like the parts of human bodies.

BODY PARTS

Skeleton: Robots have a frame that suits what they are designed to do. Delicate flying robots might be made from light plastics, but bomb-disposal robots have a thick steel frame.

Muscles: Robots generally have springs, electric motors, or hydraulic rams that act like muscles to make the robots move.

Energy: Most robots that move around have onboard batteries. Some that work in places where replacement batteries are not easy to obtain, such as on Mars, have solar panels that recharge the batteries.

Senses: Sensors on robots allow them to detect the world around them. Many have cameras on board to detect changes in light and shapes with the aid of computers.

Locomotion: Moving robots may have wheels, helicopter propellers, caterpillar tracks, or legs for getting around.

Brain: Computers act as robots' brains. Operators program the computers to tell the robots how to move and carry out tasks. Some robots have artificial intelligence, which means that they learn from changes in their environment, based on programming in their computers.

Drones are robotic flying machines that can control their own flight. Many drones take off and stay in the air using four or more spinning rotors or propellers.

CUTTING EDGE

Scientists have created artificial intelligence that allows robots to watch YouTube cooking videos and copy what they see! The robots are programmed to recognize and classify what is happening and being used in a video, and then replicate those actions using their arms.

CHAPTER 2

INDUSTRIAL ROBOTS

Many industries rely on human workers arriving at the start of the day to do their jobs and then going home. However, these people are usually part of a team that includes industrial robot workers.

ARM TYPES

There are three main types of robotic arms. Some have three sliding joints that allow the wrist of the robot to move up and down, back and forth, and in and out. Sliding arms can do simple jobs, such as squirting glue. Some robotic arms have three rotating joints a little like shoulder joints that can move more than sliding arms. The third type of robotic arm has six joints, which allow them to reach farther and work from all sides of an object. These can do complicated tasks, such as painting all the surfaces of an object.

BIONICS

Scientists have developed a flexible robotic arm with an **end effector** (see right) gentle enough to pick up an egg without breaking it! The Bionic Handling Assistant was modeled on an elephant's trunk. The arm is lightweight and flexible and is made from twisting plastic chambers that fill with air to move the arm. The arm deflates and softens if there is a collision.

The end effector on this pick and place robotic arm is a set of suckers to stick to cartons so the arm can move them from one place to another.

END EFFECTORS

Robotic arms do different jobs with different "hands," or end effectors. Some look a little like simple human hands, with fingers that grasp and grip objects. Other end effectors are tools such as pliers, drills, paint-spraying nozzles, cutters, or fire extinguishers. The action of an end effector is controlled by its sensors. For example, a robot can screw on a bottle lid to the right tightness endlessly until it runs out of bottles or there is a power outage. Some industrial robotic arms are incredibly strong: the Kuka Titan arm can reach more than 9 feet (3 m) and lift 1.1 tons (1 mt). However, others are designed for much more delicate work, such as soldering electronic **computer chips** or packing drugs into capsules.

More than half of the world's robots work in automobile factories. They are involved in all stages of putting together brand new vehicles. The process always begins with putting together panels to make body shells.

BUILDING A CAR WITH ROBOTS

Body shop: Hundreds of robotic arms work in teams of up to eight. They weld together each body shell in modern plants. Their end effectors heat up to melt together and join panels at very precise points. Each body shell has up to 6,000 weld points, and their position and strength are checked using special laser cameras on the arms.

Paint shop: Robotic arms with spray painting end effectors apply up to 10 coats of paint to the shell. The arms' movements are programmed into computers to make each covering of paint the thickness of a human hair. There are no paint drips or ripples. The paint shop is sealed so dust does not stick to the wet paint. The sealing also protects the operators—breathing in paint fumes is harmful for people, but no problem for the robot painters.

Assembly: Humans do most of the assembly of an automobile, from fitting engines to adding electronics and wheels, but they have the help of robots to ease their work. For example, Robo-glove looks like a ski glove, but has small motors inside so the person wearing it can apply 20 pounds (9 kg) of gripping power. They can then move tools with little effort. In some plants, humanoid robots with two arms can independently carry out tasks, such as fitting windshields.

Robotic arms grip and manipulate car body panels, which will be welded by other robots into complete car shells.

HENRY FORD

Henry Ford (1863–1947) devised the first assembly line. Instead of doing different jobs to make one car at a time, workers stayed in one place and did a specialist job, such as attaching the engine. Trolleys carried each partially finished automobile from one worker to the next. The assembly line cut the time for assembling a car from half a day to 1.5 hours!

You would be almost guaranteed to spot robots in action in a modern automobile plant. However, they are not restricted to this industry. Robotic technology is already in regular use in a wide range of industries.

ENERGY

Coal is the major energy resource for making power worldwide, yet coal mining is heavy, dangerous work for miners. That is why robots are used in this industry. The biggest robots on Earth weigh 3,800 tons (3,500 mt) and move along exposed coal seams, scooping up tens of tons of coal at a time. Their movements are controlled by computers.

ROBOTS ON THE FARM

Farmers use robots to reduce the need for large numbers of farm laborers. Automated fruit pickers have arms with cameras that

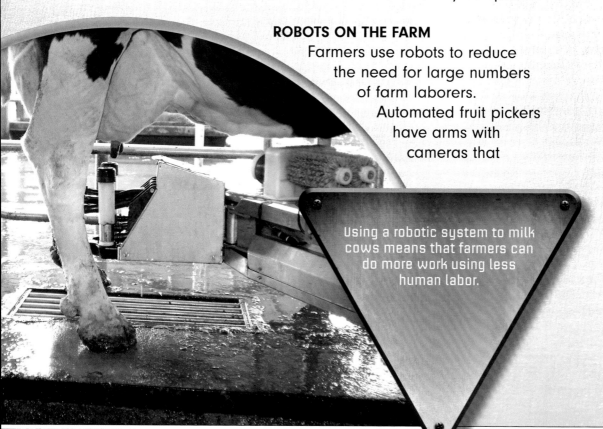

Using a robotic system to milk cows means that farmers can do more work using less human labor.

SOLAR ROBOTS

Many sunny regions, such as the Middle East and North Africa, are beginning to meet their power needs using solar farms. There, hundreds or thousands of solar panels convert the energy in sunlight into electricity. Panels produce less power if covered with dust, so scientists have developed robot panel cleaners to keep them working at their best. These have rotating brushes to clean the panel surfaces, and the robots can even climb between panels to clean them.

detect whether apples are the right color to pick. If so, sucking cones remove the fruit and gently place them into trays. Dairy farmers often use robot milking parlors. When a cow walks into a stall in the milking parlor to feed, a laser-guided robotic arm moves in to collect milk. Each cow has a chip that the robot recognizes and individually adjusts the position of the suckers to locate the cow's teats. The arm cleans the teats and pumps out the milk.

WAREHOUSES

It is becoming more and more common to do our shopping online instead of going to stores. Hit the "place order" button on a computer, and it can put robots to work in huge warehouses. Robots race along the aisles to find the ordered items, following routes made from computerized barcode stickers on the floor. The robots carry the items to people at workstations for sorting and packing, avoiding bumping into each other by using sensors.

Would you like to crawl across wind turbine blades in search of cracks, or wade through long sewers or gas pipes in search of blockages or rust? These are just some of the industrial settings that are too dangerous or too expensive for human workers.

SPOTTING DANGER SIGNS

Robot inspectors have cameras so that operators can view what they encounter. They also have other sensors, such as **infrared** or **sonar**, which can detect things we cannot spot with human eyes. On railroad tracks, robots can detect when tracks are out of alignment. Similarly, robots can climb dam walls and can see through concrete to spot any signs of damage. Wind turbine blades can rise 400 feet (120 m) up into the air, but robots can grip on to the turbine as they climb it using powerful magnets, even while the turbine blades are spinning. The robots move over the blade surface in search of damage.

RADIATION

Robotic arms are widely used in the **nuclear** power industry to handle nuclear fuel in reactors and to remove waste for safe storage. Nuclear waste produces **radiation** that can damage body tissue. Accidents in reactors can release deadly amounts of radiation. Wheeled robot inspectors were used in Japan in 2011 during the Fukushima nuclear power plant accident. They used sensors to measure radiation levels and take images of the internal structure, so experts could assess the damage. An industrial cleaning robot with a spraying end effector on its arm sprayed dry ice at high pressure onto surfaces to scrub off radioactive dust, and then it sucked up the waste.

Snakebots are so flexible that they can squeeze through small gaps, lie down or stand up, and coil around things in order to inspect their surroundings.

SNAKEBOT

Snakebots are robots that crawl like snakes and can squeeze into small gaps. Thesbot is a Japanese snakebot that has hinged sections and joints with ball-shaped wheels. The hinges move the sections so that they press against the insides of pipes the bot moves through. Thesbot can fit inside pipes just 3 inches (75 mm) in diameter to spot any damage.

CHAPTER 3

ROBOTICS IN SPACE

Robotic machines are a vital part of space exploration because space is a difficult place for humans to be, particularly for long periods of time.

SPACE RISKS

In space, there is no oxygen for people to breathe and temperatures can drop as low as –523 degrees Fahrenheit (-273°C). There is also dangerous radiation in space. People need enormous food and fuel supplies to travel in space, too. That is why people have built robotic craft to explore space.

EXPLORATION ROBOTS

Space **probes** are robot spacecraft that travel through space collecting scientific information. Most are sent to discover more about planets, comets, or other bodies. They are usually designed to reach their destination, but not to return to Earth. One of the most famous probes, *Voyager 1*, was sent to explore Jupiter. It is powered by a nuclear battery and carries cameras, magnetometers for measuring magnetic forces, and heat and movement sensors. It has sent information back to Earth as radio signals every two weeks since being launched in 1977. Orbiters are robots that are programmed to **orbit** planets. *Cassini* took pictures of Saturn's cloud formations, revealing wind speeds that are four times the strongest wind speeds on Earth.

The dish on this space robot enables radio communication with mission control on Earth. Its solar panel wings supply the power to operate in space year after year.

CUTTING EDGE

In 2022, a robot will set off to Jupiter to explore its icy moons in a mission named "JUpiter ICy moons Explorer", or JUICE. The JUICE mission will not arrive until 2030. Scientists expect the JUICE robot to study the icy crusts of Jupiter's moons with the hope of finding liquid water beneath. Humans need water to survive, so perhaps these moons could one day be home to colonies of astronauts!

Some space robots are designed to land on planets such as Mars, and usually carry robotic vehicles called **rovers** to explore them firsthand.

LANDING CRAFT

Spacecraft travel fast and their speed slows as they enter the gases around a planet. This creates **friction**, which converts movement energy into heat. When the *Viking* landers entered Mars's atmosphere, they heated up to 3,800 degrees Fahrenheit (2,100°C)! They did not melt or burn because they had thick heat shields to protect them. They also each had a parachute to slow them down as they landed.

ROVING AROUND

In 2012, a Mars lander used parachutes to slow down on its approach to Mars. It hovered over the planet's surface and carefully lowered the *Curiosity* rover, which is the size of a small car. It can travel up to 12 miles (20 km) a day on its six wheels. It has a long robotic arm with a hand-like end effector that can collect soil samples and drill into rocks. Other instruments test the atmosphere and take photos of Mars.

SPEEDY *PHILAE*

In 2014, after a 10-year journey of more than 3.7 billion miles (6 billion km), the *Rosetta* orbiter released its *Philae* lander. *Philae* was the size of a washing machine and its mission was to land on the surface of a comet that was traveling at 40,000 miles (64,000 km) per hour. Instruments on *Rosetta* found the most suitable landing spot. Despite some landing problems, *Philae* made discoveries about the comet, such as traces of chemicals on the surface similar to those found on Earth.

SkyCrane is the amazing robotic lander that can hover above Mars using thruster engines in order to lower the *Curiosity* rover safely to its surface.

Some space robots do not reach and explore planets, but instead are part of the teams that work on and outside spacecraft. Robotic arms are used for this purpose, and the biggest of all is at work on the largest spacecraft: the International Space Station (ISS).

BIGGEST ROBOTIC ARM

Canadarm 2 is a hollow carbon-fiber arm with seven joints. It is nearly 58 feet (18 m) long and can lift masses of more than 127 tons (116 mt). On Earth, the arm would collapse under its own weight, but in space, the **gravity** is far lower than on Earth, so the mass has little weight and can support itself. There are several sockets around the ISS into which either end of the arm can plug itself to gain power and link to the controlling computer. Canadarm 2 can walk, a little like a looping caterpillar, by connecting a free end to the next port, then releasing the fixed end from its starting port, and so on. The arm can attach various end effectors and is powerful enough to help visiting spacecraft dock with the ISS.

ACROBATIC HAND

Dextre is an end effector for Canadarm 2 that can do chores that astronauts usually carry out. This giant robot has two arms that are more than 12 feet (3 m) long and can rotate, move side to side, up and down, and bend backward to grip and move around. Each arm has a multitool at the end with a powered socket wrench. It also has a camera and lights so that astronaut controllers inside the ISS can see what the robot is doing. Sensors detect how much force to use, for example, in tightening up bolts. Sensors also help the robot carry out different tasks, such as changing heavy batteries.

Dextre on the Canadarm 2 is here being used to carefully move delicate scientific equipment from inside a spacecraft called *SpaceX Dragon* onto the ISS, high above Earth.

CUTTING EDGE

Robonaut 2 is a humanoid space robot. It has hands that move like human hands and grippers as feet, which allow it to attach to places inside the ISS. Scientists have been monitoring how well Robonaut 2 can push buttons, flip switches, and use tools that people normally operate. Future robonauts could become regular members of astronaut teams, and even pilot spacecraft.

CHAPTER 4

ROBOTICS IN MEDICINE

A growing number of people, healthcare centers, and hospitals worldwide increasingly rely on robotics to improve people's health and make their lives easier.

MEDICAL STAFF

Robots can be surgeons that carry out operations or pharmacists that mix up drugs to help treat patients. They can be medics that help diagnose illnesses and laboratory technicians that help interpret tests. Robotics can greatly increase the quality of life and mobility for some patients. Robots can be programmed to always carry out work in exactly the same way without tiring and making mistakes. Imagine all the x-ray **radiographs** taken of patients in the hospital and how long it would take people to look at them. Some of this time-consuming routine work is carried out by robotic radiograph scanners, so medical experts have more time to study patients and make complicated diagnoses.

CLEAN HOSPITALS

Cleanliness is vital in hospitals to remove the microscopic germs that can make patients sick. Germs can be difficult to remove. A robot cleaner can move around a room, shining **ultraviolet light** 25,000 times more powerful than sunlight over all surfaces. After about 10 to 15 minutes, the germs are dead.

Robotic devices not only scan patients but are also used to help scan pictures, so doctors can diagnose problems and come up with medical solutions.

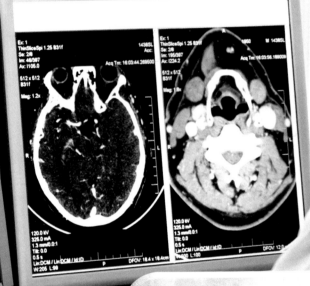

PILLCAMS

Doctors can diagnose patients by giving them robots to swallow! Pillcams are tiny capsules containing cameras that take about 50,000 photographs as they move through the digestive system. The robots send the images to a computer for a doctor to examine. In the future, robots may be able to take medicines to exactly where they are needed.

ROBOTIC SURGEONS

Today, for some surgeries, it is common for remote-controlled robots to carry out the work. Surgical robots are very expensive, yet they have several advantages over human surgeons using conventional tools.

MINIMIZING RISK

Robot surgery is minimally invasive, which means operating through smaller cuts in tissue. This reduces the amount of bleeding, speeds up the healing time, reduces the chance of infection by bacteria, and limits scarring. Robot surgery is also very precise. Surgeons move their hands and fingers to make the robot move, but at a magnified scale. So, for example, a surgeon's hand moves 1 inch (2.5 cm) to move a tiny surgical blade by 0.1 inch (2.5 mm). Accurate, complicated surgeries can become routine with robots.

SURGICAL SYSTEM

The Da Vinci is the most common surgical robot. It has carried out millions of surgeries worldwide, such as repairing damaged hearts. The part of the robot that carries out the surgery is a tower with four robotic arms that can move in any direction. Three of the arms carry tiny end effectors the width of a pencil, such as scalpels for cutting, needles for sewing stitches, or heaters to seal bleeding blood vessels. The fourth arm has endoscopes, or tiny cameras, with lights that are also held at the surgery site. The surgeon sits at a console wired to the tower and views what the endoscope "sees" on a screen. The surgeon then places their forefinger and thumb in circular controllers that are highly sensitive to movement and pressure. These send signals to a computer, which tells the three surgical arms exactly how to move, mimicking what the surgeon does.

Using robotic systems, such as the Da Vinci system, surgeons can carry out accurate, detailed surgeries.

CUTTING EDGE

Surgeon Mehran Anvari in Canada has carried out many surgeries at distances of 250 miles (400 km) using telesurgery. He operates at a console using images and communicates with nurses attending the patient during surgery via the Internet. By 2025, the U.S. Army plans to use Trauma Pods, which will be portable surgical kits, allowing telesurgery on the battlefield by surgeons at a safe distance from the action.

A robotic machine automatically prepares an intravenous (IV) medication in conditions that lessen the risk of contamination and human error.

Imagine healthcare without drugs to prevent, treat, and relieve symptoms of health complaints. Each year, doctors write out tens of billions of prescriptions, which are instructions on which drug to take, how often, and how much.

SAFER PRESCRIPTIONS
Pharmacists are experts in medicines and how they work. They prepare prescriptions for patients. Prescribing the right medicines is very important, but, unfortunately, like all humans, pharmacists can make mistakes. That is why more pharmacies are using robots to prepare prescriptions.

ROBOT DRUGSTORE

One of the most common pharmacy robotic systems is called ROBOT-Rx. It is a sealed room that contains thousands of drugs loaded onto racks in packets. Each drug type has a specific barcode. Doctors write a prescription, which has a barcode for the patient, too. ROBOT-Rx translates the prescription into a series of requests for each drug's barcode. A robotic arm locates and picks these drugs from the racks and puts them into a small box. This is emptied and sealed into an envelope, which emerges from the room on a conveyor belt and can be taken to patients. Sealing the room prevents people from taking drugs they should not.

MIXING MATTERS

Other robots specialize in mixing drugs to be given to patients as IV liquids through needles into their blood system. It is complicated to make the right mixes of some drugs; the IV liquid can become contaminated with other drugs or germs, and drugs are often wasted during mixing. Robot IV systems automatically calculate exactly the right mixes, at high speed and in sterile conditions.

LAB WORKERS

Fake medicines are a global problem. People who take these may become sicker. In one week, in 2015, police seized more than 20 million fake medicines worldwide. In medical laboratories, pharmacists use robots to identify these medicines. Robots work fast: in 1 minute they can analyze the chemicals present in 3,000 samples of different medicines!

Robotics helps people with missing or damaged limbs, organs, or other body parts. Bionic parts are those that copy natural functions using electronics and engineering.

LOCOMOTION

When someone has an accident and suffers a back injury, they may be unable to walk. Exosuits are robotic exoskeletons that people wear to help operate their legs. The ReWalk exosuit is a brace attached to the lower body. When the wearer shifts their balance, sensors in the exosuit measure the change in position. They then operate motors that bend the knee or rotate the hip joints, allowing the wearer to take a step forward. The motors are powered and controlled by a battery and computer in a backpack.

ROBOT HANDS

People can now use bionic hands. These are usually myoelectric. This means that electrical signals, from muscles in the remaining part of the arm, travel to sensors inside the bionic hand and make the joint motors move. The BeBionic hand

CUTTING EDGE

People with autism have difficulty in relating to others, for example, by misinterpreting their facial expressions. Zeno is a robot that helps autistic children learn what different expressions mean by repeating them over and over. It has a bionic face made of a type of plastic that looks and feels like human skin. It is programmed to produce 10 expressions when the skin is pulled in or pushed out by motors.

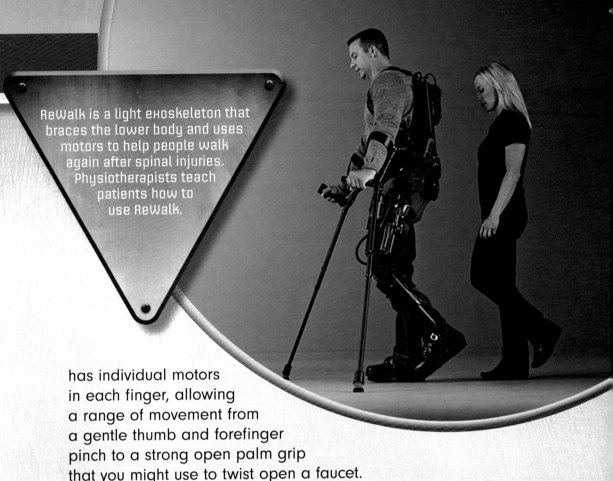

ReWalk is a light exoskeleton that braces the lower body and uses motors to help people walk again after spinal injuries. Physiotherapists teach patients how to use ReWalk.

has individual motors in each finger, allowing a range of movement from a gentle thumb and forefinger pinch to a strong open palm grip that you might use to twist open a faucet.

REGAINING SIGHT

In 2015, a man with vision loss had the first-ever bionic eye implant. He had surgery on the back of his eye to implant, or fit, a bionic retina. His glasses contained a video camera to convert what it saw into electrical pulses. Wireless messages from the glasses sent the pulses to the retina, which changed them into nerve messages, which traveled from the eye to the brain. The brain converted the messages into images that the man saw. At present, the images patients see with implants are grainy, but in the future, many people with vision loss should be able to see clearly with the help of robotics.

CHAPTER 5

ROBOTICS UNDERWATER

More than two-thirds of our planet is covered with water, hiding a wealth of living things including buried resources, shipwrecks, and other mysteries.

UNDERWATER CHALLENGES

Humans cannot breathe underwater and would be instantly killed by the massive water pressure in the deep ocean. Many underwater missions are carried out by robots called **remote operated vehicles (ROVs)**.

THE ROV

ROVs have many parts in common. They all have a group of cables called an umbilical. This passes data between the operator's computer and the ROV, supplies power to the ROV's motors, and tethers, or holds, the ROV to the ship. In the ROV's frame, there are gas-filled tanks or foam filled with air bubbles to keep the ROV from sinking. ROVs have thrusters, which are usually propellers or pumps that push back water to make the ROV move forward or change direction. ROVs have jointed arms with various end effectors such as grippers, cutters, and collecting boxes to do different underwater jobs. Video cameras aided by bright lights monitor what is around the ROV, and operators see this on screens on board the ship.

PRESSURE

The pressure from air on a person at sea level is one atmosphere, which is around 15 pounds per square inch (1.1 kg per sq cm). For every 33 feet (10 m) they travel underwater, water pressure increases by another atmosphere. So, at the deepest point in the ocean of 7 miles (11 km), the pressure is 1,100 atmospheres. At this depth, you would feel as if you were supporting the weight of 100 elephants standing on your head!

You can see the cameras and lights at the front, blue thrusters at the side, and the umbilical at the rear of this ROV.

If you go online on a smartphone, laptop, or television, then you are probably benefitting from the work of ROVs on the ocean floor laying data cables. In many ocean industries, ROVs are regular members of the teams of workers and are routinely used for a variety of tasks.

LAYING CABLES

Submarine cables for communications are laid out in straight lines with the help of ROV trenchers. These ROVs move along the ocean floor, making trenches for the cables. On some ocean floors, they use high-pressure water to blast sediment (tiny pieces of sand, shell, or soil) out of the way. However, on rocky floors, they use cutters similar to chainsaws. Other ROVs are used to explore airplane wreck sites.

OIL AND GAS

Most underwater robots are at work in the oil and gas industry. Drilling companies now operate in extremely deep ocean water to access oil and gas from rock beneath the ocean floor. Large, work-class ROVS have powerful

CUTTING EDGE

Oil spills cause great environmental damage, including killing ocean wildlife and polluting coastlines. Some modern ROVs swim beneath oil slicks and use sonar to measure their thickness. Other ROVs can move through the oil slick, and as they do so, they suck in and spin the oily water. This separates the oil from the water, and the oil is then collected in plastic containers.

Oil pollution can have devastating impacts on coastlines, but robotic machines can help prevent and clean up oil spills.

arms to help build the huge rigs needed to make drilling possible. These ROVs are used to replace worn out drill tips with newer, sharper ones. They are also used to install huge valves called blowout preventers, or BOPs, at the top of wells. The BOPs control the speed at which the high-pressure oil flows to the surface. Some small ROVs have large cameras. They are sometimes called flying eyeballs! These ROVs are used to inspect the condition of the rig, oil and gas pipes, and other parts.

In your nearest ocean, there are likely to be underwater robots at work that have no umbilicals or human control. These are **autonomous underwater vehicles (AUVs)** with battery-powered motors. AUVs are free to roam the oceans without being connected to a ship.

UNDERWATER GLIDERS

Many AUVs look a little like torpedoes or gliders, with wings for stability and tail fins that angle up or down to adjust their direction. They have a single propeller and are shaped to move quickly through the water. These AUVs keep moving, gathering data as they travel. Onboard sensors detect temperature, saltiness, and how much sediment is in the water in particular parts of the oceans. Scientists use this information to figure out how the oceans affect the world's climates. AUVs also have sonar equipment that measures the water depth and shape of the ocean floor.

AUTONOMOUS CRAFT

Many AUVs navigate themselves by using beacons on the ocean floor that make repeating sounds. An onboard computer is programmed with a route the AUV follows. The AUV constantly compares its position in the water with the network of beacons, and then adjusts its route. However, some AUVs can change their own course without programming. They are fitted with sensors that detect the amounts of particular polluting chemicals in the water. When one sensor detects more on one side of the AUV than another, the AUV may change direction so it moves to the strongest concentration of pollution in the water to find the pollution source.

ROBOTS ON ICE

AUVs help monitor global warming. At Earth's poles, scientists measure ice thickness. The SeaBED robot has two 6-foot (2 m) hulls packed with upward-pointing sonar devices that ping off the underside of the ice. It moves back and forth, checking ice depth over large areas. The ice maps made by the AUV are used to track changes in the ice cover on our planet.

The AUV Odyssey is lowered into very cold water through a hole in the ice. Using AUVs to carry out work in such challenging conditions is safer than using human divers.

CHAPTER 6

MILITARY AND POLICE ROBOTICS

Imagine a future in which robots patrol city streets and go to war. We are a long way from robot armies and police forces, but both use robotics in situations too dangerous for people or in which it is more convenient to use a robot.

ALL-TERRAIN VEHICLES

Many military robots are unmanned ground vehicles (UGVs). These are radio-controlled vehicles that have small wheels or caterpillar tracks. Operators control UGVs using touch-sensitive tablets or handsets. At a safe distance from a hazardous situation, operators can see where they are moving their robot and what it has found on a computer wirelessly linked to a video camera mounted on the front of the UGV.

PORTABLE UGVS

The advantage of portable robots is that people can easily carry them to where they are needed. They are also small enough to get to places that people cannot. The smallest robots that do this type of work include Throwbots. These are small robots shaped like dumb-bells, with a wheel at either end. Throwbots are tough enough to be thrown into a dangerous situation. When they land, they can be moved by remote control. The Throwbot then begins filming.

Big Dog can carry up to 400 pounds (180 kg) of weapons, shelter, food, and other equipment on its four legs.

CUTTING EDGE

Caterpillar tracks struggle over rough, rocky ground, but UGVs with legs do not. Big Dog is the most famous walking UGV. It is the size of a large dog and is designed to carry loads over long distances for soldiers moving on foot. It has laser sensors that automatically detect large obstacles. Big Dog adjusts its stride to move around them. This UGV can only walk, whereas the Cheetah UGV can run at 29 miles (47 km) per hour!

Military and security forces use tough UGVs. These robots carry out dangerous and difficult work while police officers and soldiers remain at a safe distance.

ROBOTANK

The biggest UGVs are robotic tanks weighing several tons, which can be fitted with a variety of attachments. Heavy metal blades at the front are used to shift obstacles, and water cannons can be used to spray crowds of rioters with water in order to clear streets. Large UGVs are often used by soldiers to help them storm buildings to rescue hostages or corner dangerous criminals. A long robotic arm with a hydraulic jaw can demolish and remove bricks, metal, and wood so that the soldiers can get inside buildings.

MINE ROBOTS

One of the main uses for UGVs is to deal with unexploded bombs. The UGV moves to a place where a bomb is known to be hidden. It is often fitted with an "electronic nose" of sensors that smell the chemicals in explosives. Dogs and rats can be trained to smell explosives, but UGVs are much more sensitive. They can detect one part of explosive chemical in 1 million billion parts of air. Computers compare the chemicals with a database of bomb smells, so experts can identify the danger. The UGV may then safely explode the bomb. In fields of landmines, or buried explosive devices, it would take too long to detect each mine individually, so the toughest UGVs take a different approach: they simply drive over them!

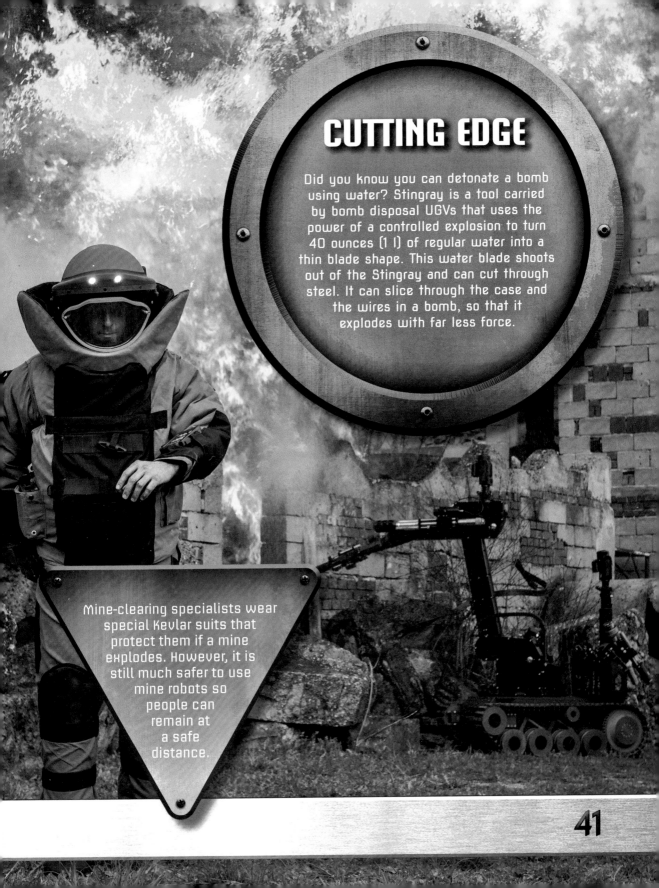

CUTTING EDGE

Did you know you can detonate a bomb using water? Stingray is a tool carried by bomb disposal UGVs that uses the power of a controlled explosion to turn 40 ounces (1 l) of regular water into a thin blade shape. This water blade shoots out of the Stingray and can cut through steel. It can slice through the case and the wires in a bomb, so that it explodes with far less force.

Mine-clearing specialists wear special Kevlar suits that protect them if a mine explodes. However, it is still much safer to use mine robots so people can remain at a safe distance.

Flying robotic machines are called unmanned aerial vehicles (UAVs), or drones. They are useful for locating criminal activity, spying on enemy forces, and for springing attacks on the enemy.

ROBOCOPTERS

The smallest drones are usually up to the size of a suitcase and are multicopters, which means that they have several spinning propellers. These are built into a frame that also supports a camera and other sensors, plus a battery to power the motors. Multicopter drones move by speeding up or slowing down different sets of propellers. An inbuilt computer called a flight controller controls this motion. The controller uses data from onboard sensors that estimate the UAV's position and angle in the air. While hovering, a drone can feed video images back to controllers on the ground. Some drones also have a thermal imaging sensor that detects heat given off by people so they can be spotted in the dark.

CUTTING EDGE

The U.S. Navy has been testing drones that can swarm like locusts! These are fired from cannons. Once in the air, they unfold their wings, and their tiny inbuilt jet engines start up. Each drone has sensors that can detect other nearby drones and mimic their flight patterns, so that tens of drones can fly in formation. If one drone is programmed to aim for a target, then the others will follow and do the same!

PILOTLESS AIRPLANES

Multicopter drones are dwarfed by jet-powered UAVs the size and shape of airplanes. The pilots of these remarkable robotic machines sit at computer control stations and never face the danger of being shot down by enemies. The Global Hawk UAV can fly at 50,000 feet (15,240 m) in the air for 32 hours at a time, taking images of the ground below. The Reaper is built for fast attack. It can fly at 290 miles (470 km) per hour and carry missiles and bombs. Unlike these drones, the X-47B drone can almost fly itself. It has a route programmed into its flight controller, but can also fly autonomously by adjusting its route based on readings from sensors, thereby avoiding collisions.

Flying robots can help police forces spot crimes in progress from the air, locate and identify people who may be a danger to others, and also help find missing people.

Robotics have already transformed our world. They have made work in industry safer and enabled highly accurate surgery and drug preparation. Robotic craft have made it possible to explore space and the oceans in greater detail than ever before. And robotics is helping security and military forces to make the world safer. However, robotic devices have only been in use since the 1980s. Just imagine how widespread they will be in the future.

NO DRIVER!

Could driverless cars be on the roads someday? Google self-driving cars have detailed street maps programmed into their computers and use information from sensors in a bump on their roofs to navigate. They also sense the position and movement directions of potential obstructions, such as cyclists and other vehicles, so they can avoid collisions. Google cars have been in testing since 2009 and could hit real streets sometime soon.

DRONE DELIVERIES

In the future, drones will have even wider uses. Amazon, the enormous mail order business, is planning a fleet of drones that can carry packages up to 4.4 pounds (2 kg) to postal addresses in a service called Prime Air. Drones are already used to monitor endangered species, pest damage in crop fields, and collect data to make maps. Scientists are also designing mini-drones to carry out the work of bees in **pollinating** food crop plants. Bees are under threat from farming chemicals and other bugs. One day, robobees with flapping wings could be programmed to swarm in places with lots of flowers, hover, and collect pollen to give bees a helping hand.

In the future, could autonomous humanoid robots be living and working beside us in homes, schools, factories, gyms, malls, and streets?

THE FUTURE

For future robots to become more autonomous, they need more complex programming to help them navigate the world around them. They need more powerful processing and better batteries that can store more power to keep going for longer. And lastly, if robots could also learn what to do in an unexpected event, the applications for robotics are almost limitless!

GLOSSARY

automatic underwater vehicles (AUVs) robots that work underwater without being controlled by operators

computer chips small slices of silicon containing electronic circuits

data information

drone a remote-controlled pilotless aircraft

end effector a device at the end of a robotic arm, which is used to do work

friction a force produced when one surface moves over another

gravity the force that makes things fall toward Earth

infrared rays of light that cannot be seen

nuclear of or relating to the release of powerful energy from certain materials

orbit the path one object in space takes around another

pollinating moving pollen between flowers to make seeds develop

pressure a pushing force

probes unmanned spacecraft

radiation the release of energy as waves or particles

radiographs images of the inside of patients taken using x-ray machines

remote operated vehicles (ROVs) remote-controlled underwater robots

rovers robots transported by spacecraft that move on the surface of other planets to explore them

sonar a system that uses sound waves to find and figure out the location, size, and movement of underwater objects

ultraviolet light a type of invisible light

FOR MORE INFORMATION

BOOKS

Ceceri, Kathy. *Robotics. Discover the Science and Technology of the Future with 20 Projects* (Build It Yourself). White River Junction, VT: Nomad Press, 2012.

Hayes, Susan. *Really? Robots.* New York, NY: Scholastic Nonfiction, 2015.

Shulman, Mark. *TIME For Kids Explorers: Robots.* New York, NY: Time for Kids, 2014.

Swanson, Jennifer. *Everything Robotics* (National Geographic Kids). Washington, D.C.: National Geographic Children's Books, 2016.

WEBSITES

Read all about Nao, a mini-humanoid robot at:
www.aldebaran.com/en/humanoid-robot/nao-robot

Discover some cutting-edge robots by visiting the websites of robotic laboratories such as:
www.csail.mit.edu and robotics.usc.edu

A brief history of robots can be found at:
idahoptv.org/sciencetrek/topics/robots/facts.cfm

Meet some robotic scientists at:
robotics.nasa.gov/students/robotics.php

INDEX